ØROP

ØROP

Renaud Camus

Translated by Ethan Rundell

VAUBAN
BOOKS

Vauban Books is an imprint of Redoubt Press, LLC

Front cover illustration, Renaud Camus, *Le Jour ni l'Heure*, Svanemølleværket, Copenhagen, Saturday, August 1st, 2009, 12:10:45

Cover and Interior Design: Robert Kern, TIPS Publishing Services, Carrboro, NC

ISBN 979-8-9887399-2-0 (paperback)

Vauban Books
PO Box 508
Blowing Rock, NC 28605
www.vaubanbooks.com

27 26 25 24 1 2 3 4

For Théodore,

on the occasion of his ninth birthday

The tragedies that had Copenhagen as their stage in early 2015, and above all the investigations, inquiries, and upheavals that ensued, brought to light a hitherto unpublished fairy tale by Hans Christian Andersen, one that is unfortunately incomplete, either because its end was never written or because it remains to be found. It seems the author intended to call this tale Ørop, the first letter being the slashed O, as in Danish, which is more or less pronounced -yur.

"But he hasn't got anything on,"
a little child said.

Once upon a time, at the far end of a continent, on a jagged peninsula with its own peninsulas, islands, bays, straits, there was a crowded empire called Ørop.*

In the days when its old people were still children, Ørop had known appalling crimes and calamities: wars, massacres, indeed exterminations, devastation without precedent. In these abominations, perpetrators and victims were obviously quite distinct. Even so, the empire felt, as

* On March 15th, 2015, this fragmentary fairy tale was read before the Assises de la liberté d'expression, a conference hosted by Riposte laïque and Résistance républicaine at the Espace Jean Monnet, in Rungis, France.

did many of its subjects, as if it alternately (and perhaps simultaneously) belonged to both of these categories. It did not really know which was the most unpleasant to live with.

"Never again!": that, in any case, was Ørop's firm resolution. Not for all the world would people once again have to go through what they had already gone through.

So as to be quite sure that the horror would not be repeated, however, that the darkest hours would not be relived, that the eternal return would once and for all be stopped in its tracks, Ørop's masters had found but one way: it was necessary to exit history, but without saying so (for to say as much would amount to an historical fact—an immediate contradiction—and the new era would thus get off to a bad start).

It would thus be claimed that nothing happened anymore, not even time itself. One would be alive, but one would be dead. Much like a doctor who, in order to totally root out the dreadful disease eating away at his patient, surgically removes not just the diseased tissue, but, little by little and as a matter of precaution, all vital functions. The patient is cured, but he no longer exists. No more brain, no more eyes, no more heart, no more anger, no more stomach, no more loins, no more legs, no more ambition, no more dignity, no more virility, no more anything.

One talked about this and that in Ørop, but it was only to kill time. Retirement pensions and who would pay for them were thus a matter of great concern. Indeed, as the nominal form of the verb *to retire*, itself a close synonym of *to retreat*, retirement was seen as the Øropean moment par excellence. To disappear: that was the ideal. To take no part in the business of the world. To kill time.

Laws were diligently passed so that men might marry men, women marry women, sons have children with their mothers without anyone being able to say a word about it. That, or yet more doggedly, teaching was reformed. At regular intervals every year, the education system was utterly remade, each time by cutting back the portion of the curriculum reserved for the most classical subjects: dead languages, mythology, rhetoric, literature, history, in short everything that would have required one to speak of the past. It was a matter of ensuring that school would be less and less school. Indeed, that was the goal to be achieved in all domains, the supreme ambition, the great objective of the powerful Ministry of Deconstruction: to see to it that living creatures and things were less and less what they were. Livestock, for example, no longer ever saw grass or sky, nor knew the joy of the fields, with the result that, like everything else, they came to resemble objects, manufactured products that one might exchange at will. Even sex came to be seen as an unduly clear-cut distinction between beings. That nothing and no one, not even the empire itself, be quite distinctly something or someone: that, it was thought, was the price of peace.

School was thus no longer school, marriage was no longer marriage, family was no longer family, children were no longer children, men were no longer men, women were no longer women, fruits and vegetables no longer had any flavor. And since everyone talked to themselves in the streets, it was no longer possible to recognize madmen. There was no more countryside because every year the suburbs devoured entire swaths of it. And since they also devoured the cities, soon everything became suburb: an endless sideline of life, something indefinable and bland, which managed to be neither the thing nor its opposite.

The French were of course no longer French, the Germans no longer German, even the Danes were no longer really Danes. Between to be and not to be, Ørop had made its choice. As one was reminded at every intersection and on the wrappers of cigarette packs: attention, living can kill! To be is the start of every danger. Even words, embarrassed as they would have been by any too precise meaning, no longer meant anything, and meaning became like a runny cheese, spilling out of itself. But since runny cheeses were banned by the imperial government and by the legislatures that meddled in everything the better to become aware of nothing, the Øropeans had not the least suspicion of all the deprivations of being and of meaning that were inflicted upon them for their own good.

If I say that laws were passed to kill time, this must be taken literally. Since it was no less than a question of exiting history, all new edicts and decrees had this in common: they struck at duration, heritage, the density of time; they sought to sap its frightful imperiousness, its way of standing like a giant whose feet, hips, torso, shoulders, and head cannot be taken in all at once. In Ørop, on the contrary, time lay quite flat, like Gulliver among the Lilliputians. One could even climb up on it with the help of little ladders and have family picnics on its flat stomach.

Yet families were also laid quite flat. Generations became ever less distinct from one another, and, since the disaster, all laws made a civic virtue out of undermining the authority of fathers, lineage, elders, ancestors, all of which were accused of being largely responsible for it. Indeed, family names increasingly fell out of usage, relating as they did to fathers, that is, to abolished, inverted time, to forever repudiated history. Increasingly, the inhabitants of Ørop referred to themselves solely by their first names, which, since they were theirs, had begun with them and would end with their last breath; having not been inherited, they had the singular merit of not being passed on, with the result that, like the empire, individuals also exited history, and with it settled into an everlasting and suspended present, which resumed as if by miracle from one moment to the next.

Having ever fewer surnames and ever more forenames, or pseudonyms, they had ever less identity and thus ever less responsibility. In the absence of name, lineage, race, there was no longer any honor or shame. The sense of guilt was entirely seen to by the state. Commitments no longer committed, signatures did not sign, speech was devalued like an old currency guaranteed nowhere.

For schools, the teaching of forgetting was the most important mission. Children attended them so as to carefully verify that they knew no history, that they hadn't the least inkling of the literature, music, and arts of their country, that they mastered ever fewer of its language's rules, and, above all, that they had not secretly gotten from their parents or grandparents any knowledge, memories, suspicions, regrets, manners that might have made them a danger for the empire or that might have restored them to themselves, to the awareness of time, to this history about which the empire no longer wanted to hear anything said. Something that went by this name was still vaguely taught so as to not directly run afoul of entrenched habits, but it was an intangible subject, torn from the passage of time: a diffuse assortment of facts, names, civilizational traits, which floated freely in a directionless limbo, and which in no way threatened to arouse among students the least feeling of duration, destiny, will, or loss.

To erase all heritage, impose the perpetual present, and guarantee that history not return because there would be no more history, no more past, no more centuries, the ideal of equality proved itself to be of matchless efficiency. The taste for the arts, the love of literature, the appetite for knowledge, the aspiration towards the examined life, all became deeply suspect over time. These dispositions of mind, which in the past had been highly esteemed and honored, were now regarded as affectations, superstitions, attempts at a dubious social magic, as the great wits of the capital put it: so many shameful attempts to reestablish or maintain hierarchies relating to duration, and that were to be dismissed as such. Since aspirations of this type were suspected of being linked with heritage, with lineages, with the slow work of families (or, worse yet, just *some* of them) to become intimately acquainted with beauty and intelligence, they were accused of representing a challenge to equality, an illicit privilege, indeed an expression of *contempt* on the part of those once privileged by fate vis-à-vis those who would today lay claim to its favor. Therefore, due to the presumed relationship between these inclinations and the accident of birth, and thus the past, and thus reviled history, they were criticized as a humiliation for those who did not profess them.

Stupefaction thus advanced in all comfort, and even a little boastfully, adorning itself in all the masks of virtue and justice. It began by imposing its music, its entertainments, its games, its leisure activities, its language, its ways of being and of seeing; and it demanded, in the name of equality, not just that they be everywhere present, that no nook or cranny escape them, that no sanctuary hold out against them, but also that in all places they be received on a footing of strict equality with the highest and most time-proven forms of reflection and artistic creation. In this regime, mundane genres and vulgar concerns wasted no time in seizing control of the entire space into which they had been introduced as highly encouraged newcomers; and from these spaces they drove out more refined interests, constantly suspected, as we have just seen, of having shameful dealings with time. While there was some foundation to these suspicions, while these learned inclinations did indeed evince a great deal of interest in and respect for time, the latter hardly returned the favor, for, as it passed, there were ever fewer people to share them and would soon be none at all. There was no longer an audience for the things of the mind. Bookstores closed by the hundreds, and, in the stalls of old concert halls, only a few elderly people were to be counted here and there, on their way to the grave.

In its happiest periods, the empire had formerly seen to it that education permit some, chosen for their thirst for knowledge and being, to lift themselves to greater knowledge and material comfort, greater self-awareness and freedom. But the exit from history and the rejection of heritage had inverted this movement. It was no longer at all a question, as before, of the best or most industrious joining the ranks of those privileged by education or the mind; to the contrary, it was now for the latter to renounce everything they owed to the labor of time, to the work of their fathers, or to the benefits of their leisure, to their own permeation by the frequentation of books, painting, travel. Since history was abolished, life and its lessons resumed each morning at the first line of the first page of the first volume. The ideal of the Øropeans—and they did not lose hope that science and law would soon permit its realization—was to beget themselves, to no longer owe anything to what preceded them.

Soon, people would no longer know that there had been centuries. They were already unaware of what each of them might have seen, experienced, and suffered over the course of its length; and, for most subjects of the emperor, the order in which they succeeded one another was unclear.

The incessant return of everything to its beginning, of all knowledge to its discovery, of all discourse to its infancy—this perpetual *da capo*, as the musicians had formerly called it, in regards to an entirely different subject, in a language that was no longer understood, indeed no more so than was their music—in short, this continuous *reset* to speak as one spoke, made children the secret kings of this ever-new society. Brand-new inhabitants, by definition, of a brand-new world, or one that wished to think of itself as such, they drew profit and esteem from their status as experts of the unknown, which no memory was likely to trouble. They thus spoke to their parents and their schoolmasters, who had long since stopped mastering anything, with a great deal of curt authority, tinged with condescending irony, in which a contemptuous and sometimes cheerful pity could be detected.

As the recognized, official, and unrivaled connoisseurs of this new power, childhood, education specialists acquired tremendous power for themselves, as is only normal. Since they owed all their prestige to the childish class, they did not neglect to say, in their singular jargon, which would soon be imposed on everyone, that the child was *at the center of the system*. And indeed, from this unstable center, pedagogy and childhood radiated across the entire society of Ørop. For several days on end, the adventures and misadventures of children's games, but played by adults of course, furnished the better part of the news in official newspapers, which were well aware that the true bloodbaths—off-field, these—did not hold the same weight in the minds of their subscribers. Under the at once familiar and stern guidance of their instructors, young people who immediately addressed them by their first names and gave them strict instructions, the elderly solemnly applied themselves to learning adolescent dances, very exotic ones ideally—Chinese, or Brazilian, or African—for the abolition of history had erased geography, and the compression of time had dissolved distance. Everything that came from elsewhere was enthusiastically worshipped, all the more sincerely as every local tradition had been obliterated on the grounds that it reeked of time.

The singers who wallowed on the ground as they dragged the empire's name through the mud, excoriating its defenders and proffering the worst insults, were directly invited to the emperor's palace so that he could make a show of his cozy relations with them and even have himself depicted in their presence by the artists of his court, as if he expected this display of good relations to revive his popularity and prestige. The same were politely invited to give talks at the country's most prestigious universities to explain the principles of their art and the reasons for their hatred to the students, who hung on their every word, finding in them subjects for their dissertations and papers. Diligence and a serious will to succeed were now exclusively reserved for childish things, for wrestling or shotput competitions, for footraces, for horse races. The most famous actors, above all the jokers among them, the buffoons, the clowns, were asked to give their opinion on the conduct of the state, as were the most famous athletes; or else they gave it without being asked, always insisting on the moral and spiritual facet of the course to be taken, about which they were considered to be the greatest, most disinterested experts. And, for the empire, the moral and spiritual facet always tended towards more self-effacement, more forgetting, less history, more passive acceptance of what was taking place, which it was only ever a question of learning to love yet more.

In this way, the reality of entertainment came to substitute for the other reality, and all the citizens became children. And indeed, they were treated as such. For instance, should they take it into their heads to not think as it was desired in high places that they should think, *education* would every time be brandished before them like a threat: always more *education*, as if they were all eight and a half years old. The legal proceedings only came later, should they refuse to learn their lessons or revise their homework, and persist in saying that time passed, that soon it would be too late.

As for the true children, the most equal among them and indeed the only ones to be so, the only ones who were not expected to become something other than what they were, those who served as model, reference point, and ideal to attain were to the contrary those who knew nothing and did not wish to know anything, or could not, because no one in their family had taken it into their heads to learn or had not had an opportunity to do so; or instead because they were strangers, if only by virtue of their language, to all that one might have been able to teach them. One had long ago given up doing so, and had even inverted the direction of instruction—out of admiration for their integrity, out of wonder that they should to this point be preserved from any perversion by knowledge, out of philosophical endearment for their artless brutality, and also a little out of fear, it must be said, because they were quick to anger. Since the good fortune of already knowing and the higher capacity for learning were (this had been proven beyond a shadow of a doubt by very serious studies, conducted by great scholars) in large measure advantages relating to accidents of birth, to inheritance, to the inscription of lineages in time, to *history* in short, accursed *history*, hatred for it and the nearly-as-intense passion shown for equality concurred in finding that such privileges should be abolished. The entire curriculum was thus designed to ensure that, in the end, the good students were perfectly brought into line with the bad ones and would know nothing more than them, nor speak better, nor write more elegantly, which would have been considered a grave breach of the imperial pedagogical ideal.

That history should be banished, and time laid quite flat necessarily implied that nothing took place, that nothing happened—in any case, nothing that was a matter of Great Politics or, *a fortiori*, the great sweep of history, of the annals of peoples, of the fate of empires. Only the sex of angels, the commendable uncertainty of which seemed an example to follow, was seen as a rightful subject of public debate; that and, to a lesser degree, economics, which ultimately came to entirely take the place of politics. For the rest, it was a question of who best held his tongue, even should it be while delivering great disquisitions day in, day out.

Those wishing to make a career for themselves in public affairs or the press had to take as their motto: *I would say even less*. And whatever office they might set their sights on in Ørop, they had to give the guarantee that they would see nothing of what was happening, that they would hear nothing of what was taking place, and above all, above all, that they would say nothing, that they would never put words to things, and even less to evils. If, despite all the precautions that had been taken, some rumblings were nevertheless heard, if the country was shaken by a dreadful cracking which the authorities were unable to completely smother or immediately sweep under the rug, the ambitious and the prudent, the true men of state, those who were going to make great careers for themselves in the official hierarchy or in the organizations that controlled and shaped opinion, stood out by their talent for translating this unpleasant noise that had pierced the silence into soothing nothingness, by their talent for reducing it to columns of numbers, elaborate excuses.

The unfortunates who did not master this particular art—the precious talent of not saying and not seeing—and who, forgetting forgetfulness, tried as they might to inform their fellow citizens that the empire was foundering, that its territory had been invaded, that its people were being replaced by other peoples, *they* were dragged through the mud and before the courts, persecuted, called all the most shameful names and those most likely to alienate all of their friends and supporters: in short, they were excluded from the community of the living, and taken for great criminals.

To be sure, there was total freedom of speech and opinion in Ørop. It was written into law and on the imperial tablets. But its natural beneficiaries, the representatives of the Press and Book Trade, remembering that it was for their benefit that this freedom had been invented and reminding all and sundry of this at every turn, felt such a strong sense of ownership towards it, such exclusive love, that they permitted no one but themselves to see to its administration and busied themselves defending their undivided right to it by any means necessary. They held every post in this sacred ministry with fierce, passionate zeal: judge, prosecutor, assistant public prosecutor, police superintendent, police officer, accuser, provocateur, informant, snitch. Those foolhardy enough to wonder out loud whether it was really true that nothing was happening soon found themselves targeted by journalists, who held hunting parties to flush them out.

And, from their backrooms, the booksellers drove out any readers daring or oblivious enough to ask whether they might by any chance have something about the truth on their shelves.

"We don't sell that sort of book!" they shouted, to be sure they were heard by informants, hacks, police officers, and judges (for they, too, were afraid of failing to exhibit sufficient enthusiasm for Right Doctrine).

Or instead, they bellowed:

We don't stock that type of author!

It sometimes happened that they would offer to order the book, but their client had already slipped away, for fear that, should he leave his name and address, he would be put on file and hunted down.

The problem for this vast empire, which had been rich and powerful, was that the rest of the world, not having the reasons it thought it had to exit history and descend from time, had not the least intention of following the example of its retreat. The other continents thought it quite ridiculous that it had given itself over to such self-immolation—that, for example, it had deliberately relieved itself of all legal and forcible means for protecting its borders, convinced as it was, officially, that nothing could happen. For Ørop no longer had an army, as it were; and the old empire saw to it that the small number of troops, weapons, and munitions that did remain to it were every day reduced yet further, judging them to be useless and expensive. It left the business of protecting it to others, who cared less and less about the empire's safety or the empire itself, exploited its weakness, profited from its fatigue, held talks with its enemies, and did not really see why, as a matter of fact, they should eternally and at great cost to themselves see to the safety of a peninsula that had once and for all decided to not make the least effort for its own survival.

Yet history, my dear children, is an old lady ever young, capricious and energetic, devilishly romantic, who bores easily and only dreams of adventures, cuts and scrapes, somber tragedies, spectacular feats, dramatic reversals, and coups d'état. She hates nothing more than evasion and retreat, above all when she senses they are organized at her expense, from distrust of her, so as to escape her grip. Ørop was thus well and truly invaded. And how could it have gone otherwise? The other nations and other peoples would have considered it too stupid to not profit from their opportunity and not conquer any part of this vacant empire, which had resisted them for centuries, which had indeed often subjugated them, and which now, by its inexplicable absence from itself, invited them to subjugate it.

The invasion, for that is what it was, took two quite different forms—or rather *three.*

The first was quite calm and occurred without fanfare: the invaders simply contented themselves, very humbly, with arriving in mass, a continuous but constantly growing influx, on old rafts loaded to the brim with men, women, old people, and children, or by way of the desert in long columns, which then hurled themselves against very high fences. In both cases, their voyage was perilous. But once they had touched the territory of Ørop, even if just with their tiptoes, everything proceeded like in one of those children's games so dear to the Øropeans, and which they mistook for reality. In these games, hardly had one's opponent reached a certain magic perimeter than they changed status, becoming completely untouchable. An avalanche of privileges and rights descended upon them. In fact, far from driving out the conquerors, as was still done in the hateful time when history existed, they were given a stipend, asked to forgive the shortcomings of their welcome, fed, provided with medical care, put up in hotels should nothing else to their liking be available. It even happened that pastors recommended (but I will quickly pass over this point with you, my dear children) that they be sent lady companions for their entertainment and diversion, and to ensure they not roam the streets, for fear they might there make a nuisance of themselves. Roam, however, they did and quite a lot, both on the doorsteps of houses and along the walls of housing projects, needing to do nothing else in order to conquer than to be there, more and more there, to be there in ever greater numbers, like those big black birds which many of their womenfolk resembled, and which, at battle's end, wait side by side, in serried ranks, at the gates, cluster in the branches of dead trees, confident in the knowledge that, whatever happens, they alone will profit.

The second form taken by the conquest was more classic: the use of murder, terror, and assassination to impose its law.

The third, for its part, was an unstable combination of the first two: a thousand-faced importunity, ranging from merely inflicting upon others one's noise, or one's pleasure in causing harm, or one's provocative, domineering gaze to aggravated violence in the commission of crime. According to the press and the authorities, when they agreed to speak about them at all, these constant attacks, major and minor alike, were little more than disputes between neighbors, problems relating to the uncertainties of travel (for the natives), an endless litany of police blotter items, of the profane, age-old, civil criminality that had since time immemorial always been the companion of poverty and forced idleness. Yet this violence served as a bridge between the two other ways of seizing hold of the country: one by sheer number, mass, proliferating presence; the other by terror. Simple discourtesy, misdemeanors, and crimes served as an apprenticeship in conquest by blood and iron. It was there that all the bomb layers and hostage takers got their start.

In any case, by virtue of the strange rules that had governed the empire since its decision to renounce time, it was understood that none of this should be said, none of this should even be seen, even though these phenomena took place in the full light of day and were as clear-cut and transparent as crystal. Wanting neither history nor trouble, the empire also did not want any enemies. At the first opportunity, Ørop baptized its conquerors *Øropeans*, and in doing so imagined it had conquered them. But the latter showed themselves to be much more honest, truthful, logical, and sensible, and, with the exception of certain moments, when they were forced to go along with the ambient madness so as to get what they wanted from the madmen, they very clearly spoke the truth: to wit, that of course they were not Øropean at all, nor had they the least desire to become such, particularly given the deep contempt they felt for such a spineless people; but that, by contrast, Ørop would soon be what they were, and would belong to them. It would take more than this admirable candor, however, this calm presentation of an agenda, to rouse the citizens of the empire from their stupefaction.

This stupefaction had a name, the poets and scholars of the imperial court had baptized it *diversity.*[1] Diversity had an idol, a very demanding and very cruel little god known as Lumpnotall.[2] Every time diversity was unduly shaken by tremors of truth and the blood flowed freely, enormous crowds rushed to the streets to parade around with their propitiatory idol, the entire people screaming in unison at its passage, *Lumpnotall! Lumpnotall!*—which in fact meant:

> *Down with the truth! As long as we live, the truth shall not pass!*

For it was known that the little god had an overpowering effect on it. Ørop's theology was a little contradictory, it is true, something that foreign observers did not fail to point out, though no heed at all was paid their objections. Discrimination was regarded with horror there, even though, from a loftier point of view, it seemed a necessary corollary of the cult of Lumpnotall. But the horror of history and the deeply ingrained habit of denying what was obvious had long since stifled all logic, as was evident from those banners on which one could read, from one side of the avenue to the other, during the large demonstrations that followed massacres:

> *Down with the effects! Long live the causes!*

> Or else:

> *Death to the consequences! Power to the reasons!*

> Or even:

> *Long live diversity! Long live intermixture!*[3]

The invaders pressed forward in ever greater numbers without encountering the least resistance, since, officially, there was no invasion. And how could there have been, since Ørop had exited history?

To merely employ such words—*invasion, invaders, conquerors*—could land you in prison or, failing that, invite the heaviest fines. And to show just how absurd it was to use such terms, responsibility for crafting the policy on mass debarkations—ironically referred to as *clandestine*[4]—was given to a woman who had herself come ashore in the same conditions a few years earlier and had in the meantime made the most of this exploit to become a government minister. To the compatriots of this high-profile clandestine, in the countries where they still remained but which they were thinking of leaving, went out the call:

> *Come one, come all, run, leave your own countries behind, come see what we can make of you!*

To the native people, nothing at all was said, for the rule was to hide everything from them. Indeed, the newly promoted minister was named Mrs. Hide-It-All. In high imperial circles, some even claimed that this was the reason she had been chosen. If a true army had appeared at its borders, Ørop would surely have asked the enemy general to please be its general as well, above all if he was called *Nothinhappenin* or *Klozyurayes*. It is true, as I have said, that Ørop had no army of its own for all intents and purposes.

One would have also sworn that this empire had no people of its own, for, with great thrusts of their chins, its chosen leaders declared a *population policy* to better ensure that the incessant flood-tide of newcomers be more evenly spread across the full extent of the imperial territory, with no nook or cranny spared, no matter how remote.

"But we're already here!" the natives might have said. "See us, see us, remember that we exist, too!"

And yet they said nothing at all, knowing only too well that their masters did not love them and planned to replace them with other peoples, whom these authorities rightly or wrongly considered more docile, more closely bound to them because indebted to them for everything, more consonant with philosophical fashion and fashion *tout court*, and less expensive. The Øropeans of Ørop were not surprised to have become invisible in the very eyes of those who governed them: they were used to holding their tongues, squeezing together, paying, making room, indeed, even of having any name forbidden them, for fear that, should they be given any leeway in referring to themselves, they might get it into their heads to start being, existing, remembering. Even the term *people* was taken from them; and while the imperial press and books written by the good souls of the court spoke of *popular* districts,[5] as one might speak of a particularly exquisite if at times difficult to swallow meal, everyone knew quite well that this was to be understood as *neighborhoods from which the people had already been driven*, *newcomer neighborhoods*. They alone had the right to say what they were, history not having been forbidden them, since they had taken no part in that of Ørop and had not experienced its darkest hours.

And yet it happened that a child appeared. It would later be known that he had been seriously ill, that his poor health had prevented him from attending school, that he had not taken the least course in forgetting. His parents were dead, his grandparents were dead, he had been raised by his great-grandparents, who were deaf and mute, so no one had been able to teach them that history no longer existed, that time now began every morning, and that what was happening was not happening. They were also very poor, could not buy books or newspapers, and only had in their poor home old textbooks, squeezed between antique gold-leafed volumes in hardcover, like those once given to good students on the day prizes were handed out. This was the child's only reading. Was it from these that he drew his inspiration? In any case, one fine day, in the middle of a crowd, in the middle of a city in Ørop, he climbed onto a chair and cried out:

[The rediscovered manuscript abruptly breaks off here.]

Endnotes

1. "Cette hébétude avait un nom… *vivre-ensemble*." A portmanteau word literally meaning "living together," "vivre-ensemble" is often used in contemporary French to evoke (and extol) the cooperative pluralism of idealized multicultural communities. While its closest equivalents in English are "social harmony" or "social cohesion," we have chosen to translate it as "diversity," as that term captures both its exhortative charge and its specific reference to multicultural situations.
2. "Padamalgam": a compound word derived from the expression "ne pas faire d'amalgame" (literally, "do not conflate"), which in France is frequently heard on the lips of politicians and journalists in the wake of terrorist attacks or particularly sordid crimes to discourage the public from too closely associating the perpetrators of violence with their ethno-cultural communities of origin. A similar phenomenon was observed in the United States in the

aftermath of September 11th, when Americans were exhorted to "stop conflating" Islam with terror and not "lump all" Muslims in with the terrorists.

3. In the original, "vive le métissage!" A term of common parlance, "métissage" ("miscegenation," "interbreeding," "race-mixing") is difficult to translate into colloquial English due to its specific political valence in French contexts. Unlike its English-language counterparts, all redolent of the legacy of scientific racism, the French term is often employed, as here, to extol the mixing of distinct human groups. In rendering it by "intermixture," we have sought to supply a neutral alternative while preserving the irony of Camus' original formulation (long live "diversity" but also its negation, the sameness produced by the universal mixing of distinct races and cultures).
4. In addition to having the same meanings as its English cognate (secret, underground, illicit), the French word "clandestine" is commonly used in both adjectival ("immigration clandestine" = "illegal immigration") and substantive ("un clandestin" = "an illegal immigrant") form in discussions relating to immigration. In rendering it "clandestine" rather than "illegal," we have here sought to preserve the irony noted by Camus: that a supposedly secret, underground, or illicit phenomenon should be taking place in the broad light of day and for all to see.
5. In the original French, "Il n'était pas jusqu'à l'appellation de *peuple* qui ne leur été ravie; et si, dans la presse impériale ou dans les ouvrages des belles âmes de la cour, il était question...

des quartiers *populaires*, tout le monde savait bien qu'il fallait comprendre: *quartiers d'où le peuple a déjà été chassé, quartier des nouveaux arrivants*." In contrast to its English cognate "popular," the French adjective "populaire" possesses strong social connotations. To say that something is "populaire" is to say that it relates to or is of the common people (for which the English adjective "working-class" is a rough but not always satisfactory approximation). What Camus is saying here, in other words, is that the meaning of the word "populaire" has been inverted or at least adulterated: it is now exclusively used to describe populations that, by virtue of their foreign origin, are precisely not part of the common people (or have replaced them). To preserve this nuance, we have in this instance deliberately opted to translate "populaire" by its faux ami, "popular."

Also available from Vauban Books

Renaud Camus, *Enemy of the Disaster: Selected Political Writings of Renaud Camus,* edited with an introduction by Louis Betty (2023)

Renaud Camus, *The Deep Murmur: Preceded by Elegy for Enoch Powell* (2024)